'Oh, dear!' Grandad sighec
think we may have hit a pr

'What do you mean?' asked Chris.

'I'm afraid it's someone else's big day that Saturday too.'

'So what?' Andrew demanded. 'What's that got to do with our Cup Final?'

'It's fixed for the same date as Elizabeth's wedding. Your cousin Lizzie's getting married that day, remember!'

Andrew and Chris Weston are devastated. They simply *can't* miss the longed-for Final against their arch-rivals, Ashford. But their mother is determined that the boys will be at the wedding and not on the football pitch. Unless a miracle happens, the boys' hopes – and the match – seem doomed.

Rob Childs is a Leicestershire teacher with many years experience of coaching and organizing school and area representative sports teams. He is the author of two previous books about the Weston brothers, THE BIG MATCH and THE BIG RACE, also published by Young Corgi Books.

Illustrated by Tim Marwood

YOUNG CORGI BOOKS

THE BIG DAY
A YOUNG CORGI BOOK 0 552 52581 2

First published in Great Britain by Young Corgi Books

PRINTING HISTORY
Young Corgi edition published 1990
Reprinted 1990

This book is set in 14/18 pt Century Schoolbook
by Colset Private Limited, Singapore.

Young Corgi Books are published by Transworld Publishers Ltd, 61-63 Uxbridge Road, Ealing, London W5 5SA, in Australia by Transworld Publishers (Australia) Pty. Ltd., 15-23 Helles Avenue, Moorebank, NSW 2170, and in New Zealand by Transworld Publishers (N.Z.) Ltd., Cnr. Moselle and Waipareira Avenues, Henderson, Auckland.

Made and printed in Great Britain by
The Guernsey Press Co. Ltd., Guernsey, Channel Islands.

With thanks to Joy for all her vital help
and support

Also by Rob Childs and
published by Young Corgi Books:

THE BIG MATCH
THE BIG RACE

BY MYSELF BOOKS are specially
selected to be suitable for beginner
readers.

THE BIG DAY

1 *Make a Date*

'GOAL!' shouted Tim Lawrence in delight as his powerful shot bulged the back of the net.

Andrew hugged his captain with excitement. 'Magic! 3-1 to us. We're in the Final now for sure.'

'Not yet, there's still a few minutes left,' Tim said, trying to calm him down. 'Just you keep our defence tight. We don't want to let them score again.'

The captain of the Danebridge Primary School football team need not have worried. They finished their Cup semi-final well on top after recovering from the shock of being 1-0 down at half-time. But it had taken two fine goals from centre-forward John Duggan early in the second half to swing the match their way.

'Congratulations, lads,' their headmaster praised them as they huddled together on the pitch afterwards. 'A well-deserved victory in the end.'

'When's the Final, Mr Jones?' Andrew blurted out. 'I can't wait.'

'I had a feeling you might be the first one to ask that, Andrew Weston,' he smiled. 'You won't have

to wait too long. It's just three weeks away now, so make sure you're free to play, everybody.'

'You bet!' Andrew laughed and then led the noisy charge back to the changing hut on their village recreation ground.

His younger brother, Chris, however, hung back shyly. He wanted so much to join the team inside, but instead waited impatiently with his grandad for them all to spill out again.

Although he had played in an earlier round of the Cup competition when regular goalkeeper Simon Garner had been ill, Chris still didn't feel quite part of the team. They were all so much older than he was.

'You should go in there and share in the fun,' Grandad suggested.

'It's all right, Grandad,' he said with a slight shrug. 'Andrew will be out any minute now.'

He scuffed his toes against the wooden steps, and Grandad could sense the boy's mixed feelings. Chris would be pleased for his brother, of course, but knew that he himself was unlikely to be picked for the Final.

He tried to cheer his grandson up. 'Well, I reckon Simon was mostly to blame for their goal today, you know. He should have held on to that ball

like you would have done, not just pushed it straight back out to their attacker.'

'Maybe, Grandad, but he did well really in the first place to stop the shot,' Chris said generously. 'He was just unlucky with the rebound, that's all.'

Privately, though, Chris rather agreed with Grandad's comment. He fancied himself a better keeper than his rival but, for now, just had to put up with the fact that Simon Garner was first choice for the school. He knew his own turn would come next season when Simon and the rest had left.

Any further brooding was rudely interrupted, however, as the door was flung open by Andrew and Tim having a friendly wrestle to see who could get down the steps first.

'Did you hear old Jonesy at the end of the match?' Andrew jeered, enjoying a rare little triumph. 'As if any of

us would be doing something else and miss the Cup Final. What a stupid thing to say!'

'When is it?' Chris asked.

'Don't you even know that yet? You should have been in the hut with us. What a laugh! Hey, Tim, are you coming round our house to play for a bit?'

'Can't. Got to get home, we're going out this afternoon. See you.'

'Well, Andrew?' said Grandad, repeating the question. 'If you won't answer your brother, tell me. I'd like to know too. I don't want to miss the match either.'

'Oh, sorry, Grandad. It's later this month, on Saturday the twenty-eighth.'

Chris saw Grandad's face fall, even though Andrew was too full of himself to notice.

'Oh, dear!' Grandad sighed heavily. 'I think we may have hit a problem, boys.'

'What do you mean?' asked Chris.

'I'm afraid it's somebody else's big day that Saturday too.'

'So what?' Andrew demanded. 'What's that got to do with our Cup Final?'

'It's fixed for the same date as

Elizabeth's wedding. Your cousin Lizzie's getting married that day, remember!'

'Oh, no!' Chris gasped. 'You're right. Mum was going on again last night about what we were going to have to wear for it.'

Andrew began to look seriously worried. 'Hey, are you two having me on or something? Because if you are, I don't think much of the joke.'

They shook their heads.

In desperation, Andrew sought a possible way out. 'Well, we've still got time to play in the morning and get cleaned up in time for church, haven't we?'

Grandad didn't know how to break the bad news gently. 'It's a morning wedding, Andrew, eleven o'clock, and I've a nasty feeling that your mum will insist that you're both there. All the arrangements were made months ago.'

The brothers looked at each other in silent horror. They simply did not know what to say.

2 *Keep It Secret*

'I'm sorry, but you're not getting out of it. You are both going to the church and that's final!'

This marked the end of another vain attempt by Andrew and Chris to persuade their mother to let them miss the wedding. Her angry words as they left the house still haunted them as they booted a ball about aimlessly on the recreation ground.

Chris wasn't even in the mood to throw himself around in goal the way he normally loved to do when they came out to practise together. 'More like she means it's *not* the Final, by the sound of it!'

Andrew snorted in disgust at the cruel double meaning of the word.

'There's got to be some way we can change her mind,' he said firmly, choosing to ignore the fact that they had pestered for days without it doing any good. 'There's just got to be. How's the team going to be able to get by without me holding the defence together?'

Usually Chris would have jumped

at the chance to mock his older brother's boastfulness. But for once he let him get away with it as Andrew slammed the ball into the wall of the hut in a flash of temper, almost splintering the rotting wooden boards.

Now did not seem a very good time to start an argument.

'It's no use,' Chris said simply instead. 'Even Grandad has failed. Mum just repeats to him what she's told us.'

'Yeah, I know, I know,' Andrew cut in, and then began mocking their mother's reasons in a high, squeaky voice. 'The boys have known about

the wedding for ages; it's not my fault their football match happens to be on the same day; we can't let Lizzie down, she'll be so disappointed if her little cousins aren't in church. . .'

Chris shrugged. There seemed nothing more they could do. Mum knew very well how much the game meant to them, but she was determined the wedding had to come first. She had even written to the headmaster to apologize and explain why they were not able to play.

'When are you going to hand that letter to Mr Jones?' he asked.

'What! Are you kidding?' Andrew yelled. 'I'm not going to – and neither are you. I've already thrown it away.'

'But. . .'

'Listen, I'm warning you. If you let on to *anybody* I can't play, you'll get thumped. Understood?'

Chris got the message all right, but still wasn't clear why it should be kept a secret. His face showed it.

'Don't look at me like that. There's still time yet, anything might happen. I'm *not* going to give up hope. Maybe Lizzie and her boyfriend will fall out or something and call it all off!'

Chris shook his head. 'It just doesn't seem fair on the rest of the

team, that's all. You know, acting as if nothing's the matter and then having to drop out at the last minute.'

Andrew flared up and angrily hoofed the ball far away into the distance. 'Not fair on them! I'm the one who's being dragged along to some stupid wedding when all my mates are playing in a Cup Final and winning a medal. What's fair about that? Why did she have to go and pick that day to get married?'

Chris gave up and trotted off to fetch the ball to let Andrew cool down a bit. As he did so, Tim and Duggie came running towards them.

By the time he returned, the three of them were already chanting the chorus of '*We're going to win the Cup!*' with Andrew's voice the loudest of them all.

'We've heard it's Ashford we're up against in the Final,' Tim added, breathlessly, when they'd finished. 'Just right for revenge.'

'Perfect,' Andrew grinned. 'They were dead lucky to beat us in the league match before Christmas.'

'Wasn't it 3-0 to them?' Chris chipped in.

'So? You weren't even there, so belt up!' Andrew glared at him, still cross. 'Anyway, they won't get a kick this

time. We'll tear 'em apart and Duggie here will score a hat-trick!'

'Yeah, with Simon in goal, you at the back, Tim in midfield and me up front, Ashford won't stand a chance.'

The boys laughed and continued to joke about what they were going to do to their opponents, ignoring Chris completely. He wondered how Andrew could carry on like he was, knowing he almost certainly wasn't going to be allowed to play when it came to the crunch.

At that point, seeing Simon approaching too, Chris decided he'd had enough. He slipped away and left them to it, doubting whether any of them would even notice.

But over the next few days Chris wasn't the only one worrying about the risk of letting the team down. Andrew was affected too, far more deeply than his brother would ever have realized.

As he had not missed a match so far this season, nobody else was used to

playing in his key position at the heart of the defence, and Andrew began to feel very bad about not giving the headmaster enough time to try and sort the problem out.

His guilty secret was proving harder and harder to bear. He knew he was in the wrong, but he just couldn't face up to the fact of not actually playing in the Final. He still hoped against hope that everything, somehow, would work out all right in the end.

If it didn't, he could only guess at the trouble he would be in.

Andrew tried to bottle up such fears inside, but finally it all became too much of a strain. His stomach was so churned up in knots that one morning in school assembly, in the middle of singing the first hymn, he suddenly felt very weak and strange.

Before he could stop himself, or make a move to leave the hall, he was spectacularly and noisily sick all over the next two rows of children standing in front of him!

And much to his teacher's great dismay, too, Andrew was then sick again back in the classroom later. Neither was John Duggan best pleased, since most of it went over his maths book.

For everybody's sake after that,

Andrew was sent home, only for him soon to notch up his own sickly hat-trick in the bedroom.

'Really, Andrew, couldn't you have dashed to the bathroom in time?' Mum scolded, beginning the unpleasant job of cleaning up the mess.

'Sorry, Mum, it just comes on me so quick. There's no warning, like.'

'Right, my lad. We'll have you to the doctor's tomorrow then to see what's the matter. I should think at least a couple of days off school will be needed to help make sure you're fit for Saturday.'

'No, no, I'm OK, really,' he began

to protest. 'Apart from being sick, that is, I mean. If I miss school, I might not even get picked for the team. . .'

Andrew tailed off, realizing what he'd said, and sank quietly back into his pillow. His mother looked at him sharply, noticing how his face seemed to have turned even paler.

'What's that got to do with it, Andrew? Mr Jones already knows that you can't play, doesn't he?'

'Well, yes, b . . . but. . .' he stumbled, trying to hide the truth.

'Good, so there's no point in worrying your head over that now, is there? What I'm talking about, of course, is getting you well again in time for Lizzie's wedding.'

Andrew gave a low groan. That was not exactly the kind of news to make him feel any better at the moment!

3 *Team News*

'Good to see you back at school, Andrew,' Mr Jones smiled. 'And just in time for the soccer practice too! I was beginning to fear we might have to rule you out for Saturday.'

Andrew forced a false grin. When Chris had suggested his sickness was a perfect excuse to get them out of their terrible fix, he had almost given in to temptation. But his desire to

play in the Final was so strong, he'd returned to school as soon as possible, still clinging to the desperate hope that Mum would back down in the end.

The other footballers were especially relieved to see Andrew charging around in the practice after school with all his usual energy and enthusiasm. He didn't dare tell them, however, that he'd been sick with nerves behind the changing hut before the start.

Chris found himself on good form, making some fine saves, but his heart wasn't really in it. He guessed he would land in hot water too when

Andrew did finally have to own up to their secret, although he felt sure there was no danger of him being chosen in place of Simon.

Even so, when Mr Jones gathered them together at the end to announce the team, Chris still couldn't help half-hoping to hear his own name, despite everything.

'To be fair,' the headmaster began, 'I've decided to keep an unchanged side from the semi-final. Likewise, the two subs are boys who also deserve to be included in the squad for helping us on our way to the Final. One of them is young Chris here. It'll do no harm at all to have a spare keeper around, just in case.'

Chris heard little else that was said. He felt too stunned, and he couldn't bring himself to look anybody in the eye for fear they would see his guilt. Instead of pleasure, a great cloud of doom settled over him, and when Andrew raced off with Tim afterwards, Chris wandered slowly across to where Grandad was waiting.

'You don't have to tell me,' Grandad said, nodding with understanding. 'I could tell what's happened by all the fuss you were getting and by the look on your face now.'

Grandad too had been hoping that somehow things might sort themselves out, but now, he reckoned, was the time to face facts. 'Don't you think Mr Jones ought to be told the truth at last?'

Chris looked up at him sharply in horror. 'I can't, Grandad, Andrew would kill me if he found out I'd blabbed.'

Grandad sighed. 'Well, suit yourself, but it's for your own good. It's different for Andrew, he'll be leaving soon and this is his last chance. You've still got a couple of years of playing in goal here to look forward to yet.'

The old man began to fill his pipe to allow Chris time to think the matter over before he continued. 'And Mr Jones may not forgive how you seemed to be prepared to let him and the school down . . . you see what I'm getting at?'

Chris did, only too well. The mere thought that he might never be allowed to play for the team again was so awful he almost burst into tears.

'It's up to you, Chris,' Grandad said gently. 'But if you decide to, don't put it off until tomorrow. It might be too late by then.'

Mr Jones was just about to get into

his car to leave when he realized that someone was standing behind him. He turned round to see it was Chris Weston – looking very upset.

'My, whatever's the matter with you? I thought after hearing the team you'd have been dancing with joy. Has somebody said something?'

Chris shook his head. 'No, that's just the trouble. Nobody's said anything and we should have done.'

Puzzled, the headmaster waited for Chris to explain what he meant.

'I'm sorry, Mr Jones, really I am. I didn't expect to be picked so I hadn't told you.'

'Told me what?'

Chris hesitated, before Grandad's warning made him continue his confession. 'It's just that I can't play on Saturday. My cousin's getting married and Mum says I have to go to church instead.'

'Oh, dear! I'm sorry to hear that, Chris. What a pity! But I'm glad you've told me now at least. Better late than never, I suppose. Hmm . . . let me see, perhaps we could still keep you as sub so you get your medal, even if you aren't actually there. . .'

He stopped suddenly as a doubt crossed his mind. 'It's a good job your mum hasn't banned Andrew from playing as well then, isn't it?'

He waited for Chris to answer and confirm that all was well regarding his brother, but the boy just hung his head in silence.

Nothing more needed to be said. The headmaster now began to see what might have been behind those recent bouts of sickness and he tried hard to control his anger in front of Chris.

As for Andrew, however, Mr Jones had plans which would make that particular young man feel really sick!

By the time everybody had gathered round at Grandad's cottage later that same evening to enjoy a family get-together before Elizabeth's wedding, Chris had still not plucked up the courage to warn Andrew about what he'd gone and done.

The two boys were sitting quietly at the back of the room, with Andrew too busy worrying about how to break his own news about the team to Mum to bother talking to his brother. Suddenly, however, he lurched forward off his stool and brought up the remains of his tea down behind the settee.

'Oh, Andrew, not again!' Mum squealed. 'I thought you'd got over all that.'

The bride-to-be immediately became

rather alarmed. 'Do you mean he's done that before this week, Aunty?'

'I'm afraid he has, many times,' she admitted.

'Well, I'm not sure I like the thought of him being horribly sick like that right in the middle of my wedding service. It'd ruin everything for me.'

As they fussed around, Lizzie made it quite clear she didn't want the risk of having a sickly little boy in church, and a white-faced Andrew could see that Mum was beginning to weaken.

He seized his chance. 'Does that mean I can play in the Final after all,

Mum, and help Danebridge win the Cup?'

She eyed him suspiciously, half-wondering whether he could in some way be making himself ill deliberately, but then sighed. 'Oh, I suppose so. You certainly can't stay at home by yourself all Saturday morning. Mind you, I fail to see how you can be fit to play football if you're not well enough to sit in church.'

Andrew was hardly able to hide his smirk when Mum said he'd better see if Mr Jones could still find a place for him in the team.

'Oh, he will, somehow, you can bet on that,' he said, slipping a wink across to Chris, who was too stunned by Andrew's cheek to say anything himself.

'What about Chris as well?' Grandad spoke up, sensing trouble ahead now that the headmaster already knew of Andrew's little game. 'Mr Jones might like to have him there too.'

But Mum quickly squashed that idea. 'Oh, no! Sorry. I'm having at least one of my sons in church with me. They're not both going to escape.'

'Tough luck, our kid,' giggled Andrew later, out of Mum's earshot. 'Funny how things work out sometimes, isn't it? I shouldn't worry, though, I don't suppose old Jonesy will mind too much when he hears you can't play. He can easily pick somebody else as sub.'

Neither of them knew it then, but Andrew was soon to be in for a nasty shock when he found out just who that somebody would be. . .

4 *All Change*

Mr Jones wasted no time in calling Andrew into his office the following day. 'I understand that you are, in fact, unable to play on Saturday.'

Andrew didn't have a chance to wonder how the headmaster knew or even start to deny it before another bombshell hit him.

'That being the case, I've already changed the team and chosen somebody else in your place.'

'No, no,' Andrew blurted out, tears springing to his eyes. 'It's OK, honest. Everything's fine now. Mum said last night I didn't have to go to the wedding. I knew she would in the end.'

'So you admit you knew you might not have been free to play?'

'Well . . . well . . . y . . . yes,' Andrew stammered, 'b . . . but. . .'

'But you decided not to tell me until it was almost too late to do anything about it. Or perhaps even leave us all in the lurch completely by just not turning up on the day itself?'

'No . . . no, it wasn't going to be like that . . . I mean. . .'

Andrew dried up, sensing it was useless to try and defend himself. After a long, heavy silence, he attempted an apology instead. 'I'm sorry, Mr Jones. It's just that I wanted to play so badly, I couldn't bear the thought that I might have to miss the match. And I can play now, really.'

'I'm sorry too, Andrew,' the headmaster replied, less sternly. 'But I have to set an example with you over this. I can't have boys putting themselves selfishly before the team like you've done, whether you meant to or not. The team and the school are more important than any single player,

whoever he might be. Remember that.'

Andrew nodded weakly.

'I'm afraid you've had to learn your lesson the hard way. However, you can count yourself very lucky that I'm still going to let you come with us – but only as a substitute. We'll have to see then if we can bring you on at some point in the game.'

It was a tremendous blow to Andrew's pride, not to mention a great shock to the rest of the team as well when they heard the news that their key central defender had been dropped. But after learning the reason why, they would only give

him back their support in return for his promise not to take it out on Chris, who by now had owned up to telling Mr Jones.

'Serves you right, really, you idiot,' Tim told Andrew, summing up their feelings. 'That's what *you* should have done in the first place!'

The Cup Final was due to kick off at half past ten in the nearby town of Selworth, half an hour before Elizabeth's wedding ceremony in Danebridge church. The two official substitutes got ready in their bedroom on the Saturday morning almost in silence, neither wanting to

watch the other dressing in such different gear to go their separate ways.

Andrew already had the team's red and white striped football kit on underneath his tracksuit, and was checking the laces and studs of his boots before leaving to travel to the match in the school minibus.

Chris meanwhile was trying, without success, not to think of all the excitement he would be missing, as he struggled into his new suit and wrestled with his unfamiliar tie.

At last they caught each other's eye. 'You're getting ready early,' Andrew began, for want of anything else to say.

Chris shrugged. 'Nothing else to do. Might as well get it over with, I suppose. And this tie will take ages!'

They exchanged a grin, their first for some time.

'No hard feelings, Andrew?'

'No hard feelings, Chris. You were right and I was wrong, and here I am

going to the match and you still have to go to a silly old wedding. If anything isn't fair, that isn't.'

'Oh, well, can't do anything about it now, I guess,' Chris sighed. 'Good luck. I hope you get on the pitch and help us win the Cup.'

'I will. How can they manage without me? The first sign of trouble and Jonesy will whip me straight on to sort everything out! He knows how much they need me really.'

They laughed and Andrew left with a joke. 'Be good in church, little brother, and don't go being sick! I'll make sure they save a medal for you as well, don't worry.'

'See you later,' Chris called after him as Andrew clattered down the stairs two at a time.

That was going to be sooner than either of them ever imagined. . .

5 *Send for the Sub*

Despite the spring sunshine, Chris stood waiting miserably outside Danebridge church, his thoughts clearly elsewhere.

'Cheer up!' Grandad said. 'It's not the end of the world. There will be plenty more Finals to come for you in the future, if I'm not very much mistaken.'

Chris managed a weak smile. 'I

hope so, Grandad. I just can't help wondering how they're getting on, that's all.'

'Aye, lad, only natural. I must say it's crossed my mind more than once too since they kicked off.' He looked at his watch. 'That was about ten minutes ago now. They'll be OK, I'm sure. And if not, well, they've always got Andrew in reserve to call on.'

Five miles away, as Grandad spoke, Andrew was already ripping off his tracksuit and preparing to get into the action. Things, sadly, had been going wrong for Danebridge right from the start.

Within the first few minutes they had missed an open goal, had their own crossbar rattled and then, worst of all, goalkeeper Simon Garner had suffered a nasty bang on the head when he dived down among flying feet to grab the ball.

The game was held up while he received attention from Mr Jones,

who was more concerned to make sure the boy was all right than whether or not he would be able to carry on.

Simon looked a bit groggy but insisted he was OK when he realized there was a danger of being taken off.

'What do you think?' asked his father.

'The best thing will be for you to take him for a check-up at the doctor's as soon as you can, just to be on the safe side,' the headmaster replied.

'Let him stay on for a while yet and see how he goes, or he'll be so disappointed.'

Against his better judgement Mr Jones agreed, but was soon regretting it. The next time the ball came his way, Simon fumbled it badly and then even let a simple back-pass slip through his hands.

'Right, that's enough,' he decided. 'I'm sorry, Mr Garner, but Simon will have to come off, for his own sake. He's obviously not quite with it. We'll just have to make do as best we can without him.'

He knew that was going to be easier said than done. But even before he could send Andrew on, Danebridge were a goal down. The headmaster had been so busy thinking about who could play in goal that he never even saw the shot go in.

'What on earth happened?' he asked Mr Lawrence, Tim's father.

'Poor old Simon dropped the ball at the centre-forward's feet, I'm afraid. Probably took his eye off it, fearing another clash. He's lost all his confidence now, I bet, not to mention his nerve.'

Mr Jones groaned. 'Right, Andrew, you're on. Go and do your stuff and make up for all the bother you've caused.'

The referee delayed the re-start while Danebridge made their changes. John Duggan reluctantly pulled on

Simon's green goalkeeper's jersey, while Andrew was able to slot straight back into his usual position. He was thrilled to be on so soon and relished the battle ahead with his team now so much up against it.

'C'mon, Duggie, do your best,' Andrew urged, knowing his friend was much better at scoring goals than trying to stop them. 'We can't let them get another.'

But they nearly did straightaway. Before the emergency goalkeeper could settle in, he was beaten by an awkward bouncing shot, only to be rescued by Tim getting back in time to kick the ball off the goal-line.

At that moment, Mr Lawrence decided that something had to be done if his son was going to have any chance of lifting the trophy at the end of the game.

'This is ridiculous,' he said. 'We have an excellent goalie as sub and he's not even here. I'm going to the church to see if I can get hold of him before it's too late. He'll be more use to us than to them, that's for sure!'

Before Mr Jones could stop him, he was gone, running off to his parked car nearby and working out how long it would take him to get there and back if he drove at top speed.

But as Mr Lawrence raced recklessly along the country roads, Duggie was fishing the ball out of the net after Ashford had taken merciless advantage of Danebridge's problems to score their second goal.

'What!' Mum exclaimed as Chris stood by her side, open-mouthed, after hearing Tim's father's amazing request. 'You're wanting to take my son away this very minute to play football?'

His sudden arrival had been equally dramatic, screeching to a halt outside the church gate where the bride's car had been expected to pull up at any moment.

'Please let him come, Mrs Weston. I know this must seem very rude of me, turning up like this out of the blue, and I apologize. But his team does desperately need him.'

Mr Lawrence was still trying to

persuade her to release Chris when Elizabeth duly appeared on the scene. As the bride walked up the path towards the church with her father, she was surprised to find a group of people blocking her way.

'What's going on?' she asked, as her bridesmaids fussed around her, all eager to make their long-awaited entrance into the crowded church.

It was left to Grandad to explain the situation and Lizzie gave a little chuckle. 'It seems I'm fated not to have my soccer-mad cousins watching me getting married,' she smiled. 'Come on, Aunty, this is supposed to be a happy day for everybody. I don't

want any long faces in church. Let him go and play, if it's so important.'

Chris's hopes soared but still Mum remained uncertain.

'But he's got all his best clothes on. . .' she began, sensing she was losing the argument.

'Don't worry, Mrs Weston,' Mr Lawrence reassured her. 'He'll be able to change when we get there.'

'Well . . . I suppose so, all right, as long as Lizzie doesn't mind. . .'

Chris gave a leap of delight. 'Thanks, Lizzie, that's great!' he cried. 'I promise I'll come next time you get married!'

They all laughed, much to Chris's embarrassment when he realized what he'd said, but Lizzie came to his rescue again. 'Don't worry, Chris, I don't intend there to be an action replay, and I can see from Grandad's

face where he would prefer to be too.'

Grandad began to make a feeble protest, but Lizzie brushed it aside. 'Go on, Grandad, off you go as well. I'm sure Chris would love to have you there in support. And now, if nobody has any objection, I'd very much like to go and join my future husband before he leaves! He must be wondering where I am.'

'We'll be back in time for the reception,' Grandad promised with a grin and a wave. 'Chris won't want to miss the food at least.'

It was only as they roared out of the village that Chris suddenly had a nasty thought. 'My boots! I haven't got any boots. Can we go back for them?'

'No time, I'm afraid,' replied Mr Lawrence. 'As it is, we'll be lucky to get you on even for the last fifteen minutes. Let's just hope and pray that's long enough to try and repair any more damage that might have been done since I left.'

6 *Say Cheese!*

Chris's sudden appearance on the touchline caused quite a stir.

Not expecting Mr Lawrence's trip to succeed, the headmaster had said nothing about it to the players at half-time.

He looked Chris up and down with a grin. 'My, you are looking smart! But now you're here, get that suit off, we need you in goal. It's amazing we're still only 2-0 down.'

The next time the ball went out of play, the Danebridge re-shuffle took place and Duggie bounded across in relief. 'Never thought I'd be so pleased to see you, little Westy! Now I can get back up in attack where I belong.'

Chris found himself quickly stripped down to his underpants before being re-dressed in his favourite green top with the black number 1 on its back. The spare shorts fitted him all right but, to his dismay, there were no boots his size.

'Sorry, Chris, you'll have to play in what you've got on,' said Mr Jones as he bundled him on to the pitch.

Chris hardly heard the cheers from the Danebridge supporters. He was too busy worrying what Mum would say if he messed up his best shoes to have any time for nerves about facing Ashford.

'Right, we can still beat this lot now we've got my kid brother in goal,' Andrew shouted, slapping Chris on the back in welcome.

In fact, it was mainly through Andrew's tremendous work in defence that Ashford had so far failed to increase their lead. Several times he had come in with vital tackles when another goal had looked likely.

The whole team now responded and

at last began to play the kind of football that everybody knew they were capable of. Quite swiftly the game took on a different pattern, with Danebridge getting on top and making Ashford fall back on defence for the first time in the match.

But then, as if to show how dangerous they could still be, Ashford suddenly put together a lightning raid. The right winger outpaced his chaser and whipped over a pinpoint cross beyond Andrew's reach, planting the ball perfectly in the centre-forward's stride for him to blast home.

Already with both their goals to his credit, he seemed certain to score his

hat-trick and clinch the Cup. But, to everybody's amazement, Dane-bridge's new young goalkeeper flung himself high to his right, arched his back and at the last possible moment somehow got his fingertips to the ball to knock it away from just underneath the crossbar.

'What an incredible save!' gasped Mr Jones. 'That looked a goal all the way.'

'It sure made my desperate dash back to Danebridge worthwhile,' Mr Lawrence said. 'Without Chris in goal that would have been curtains.'

Grandad beamed with pride, not regretting missing the wedding one little bit now. 'Well,' he said out loud to anyone who may have cared to listen. 'If that doesn't inspire them, nothing will.'

The team didn't let Chris down. Tim, his sleeves rolled up as usual in his business-like way, urged his players on to even greater efforts, refusing to let anyone give up.

They had badly missed Duggie's strength up front too for most of the match, but now one of his typical, brave challenges among a ruck of bodies helped Danebridge pull a goal back.

Winning the ball forcibly in a goal-mouth scramble, Duggie turned it smack into the path of his captain, lurking on the edge of the penalty area for just such a chance to shoot.

Tim made no mistake. He picked his spot carefully and drove the ball low and hard to the goalkeeper's left and into the far corner of the net.

Dodging all attempts to congratulate him, he immediately dashed for-

Apart from Chris at the far end of the pitch, every single player was crammed into Ashford's penalty area as Tim himself took the corner and swung it, head-high, into the goal-mouth.

Andrew's heading ability was normally only used for clearing the ball out of danger away from his own goal, but now it was seen to far more deadly effect. Circling round to try and confuse his marker, he suddenly burst clear of him as Tim struck the ball.

It could not have worked out better if they had practised it for months!

Andrew met the ball firmly with his

forehead and it sped like a guided missile into the goal, exploding into the netting before the helpless keeper could make any move to stop it.

Cheers and groans erupted from the crowd around the pitch as Andrew found himself buried and almost suffocated under a mob of red-striped shirts. It was his very first goal for the school team – and his last.

'Wow!' he gasped when given a chance to breathe. 'If that's what happens when you score, I don't think I'll dare do it again!'

There wasn't even time to re-start the game before the final whistle blew, to the great disappointment of the Ashford players who had seen victory snatched from their grasp at the last possible moment.

'When's the replay?' Andrew demanded. 'I can't wait to get at 'em again.'

'There isn't one,' Tim answered him.

'What! OK then, we'll stuff them in extra time instead. Even better! They're finished.'

'No extra time either. That's it, we're all finished now.'

Mr Jones soon confirmed what Tim had said. 'I think a draw's the fair result in the end after all our

problems early on. Nobody really deserved to lose such a marvellous game. The trophy's shared.'

Tim and the Ashford captain went up together to receive the Cup, and the applause continued as all the players were awarded their individual medals. Even Simon reported back in time with nothing worse than a headache.

The two captains then had to toss a coin to see which school would be first to keep the Cup in their trophy cabinet.

'Heads!' Tim called and watched tensely as the spinning coin hit the ground and began to roll. When it

finally flopped over, his leap of delight left nobody in any doubt about who'd been lucky.

In the middle of all the excitement, Grandad had a quiet word in the headmaster's ear.

Mr Jones nodded and then called for order. 'Right, boys, no time for celebrations here. We've thought of somewhere else even better. Come on, all of you, grab your gear or we'll be too late. Follow me!'

Puzzled, the footballers did as instructed and a convoy of parents' cars tailed behind the minibus back to Danebridge. But instead of stopping at the school, the headmaster drove on past until he reached the village church where photographs were still being taken outside.

'Everybody out!' he cried, and it was another toss-up as to who seemed the most surprised at the team's arrival, the smartly dressed wedding guests or the boys themselves in their dirty football kit.

'We've brought the Cup back for you to see,' said Grandad in an effort to explain things to an amused Lizzie. 'Because without Andrew's equalizer and Chris's brilliant goalkeeping, the team would have lost.'

'It's our way of saying thank you as well for letting your sons come and

play for the school on such a big day as this, Mrs Weston,' added Mr Jones, before pointing down to Chris's feet. 'And I'm very sorry about those. That was my fault, not his.'

She stared down at his wrecked shoes and for an awful moment Chris thought Mum was going to be very angry with him or, even worse, with the headmaster. But when she looked up, she was actually smiling. 'Never mind, he was growing out of them anyway, and I guess it *was* in a good cause. I'm just glad he didn't have to play in his new suit too!'

And so a very unusual photograph

was included in the family's wedding album. It showed the happy bride and groom surrounded by a group of excited footballers, cheerfully holding up their medals as they posed for all the clicking cameras. They were also the only school team pictures that ever featured a pair of newlyweds!

'Well done, both of you!' praised Lizzie, as Andrew and Chris stood next to her, tightly gripping the Cup. 'I'm very proud of you.'

She bent down and, to everyone's glee, asked, 'Aren't you going to give the bride a kiss then, cousins?'

They immediately went bright red with embarrassment in front of all their laughing friends. But, after each had pulled a bit of a face, they remembered how much they owed to her and leaned forward, one on either side, to kiss her on the cheeks.

Grandad chuckled and turned to Mr Jones. 'I think they'd much rather have kissed the Cup, don't you?'

THE END

THE BIG MATCH

BY ROB CHILDS
ILLUSTRATED BY TIM MARWOOD

'ACE SAVE, CHRIS!' shouted Andrew as his younger brother pushed yet another of his best shots round the post. 'You're unbeatable today.'

But will he be unbeatable when he is picked to stand in for the regular school team goalkeeper in a vital cup game against Shenby School, their main rivals? For Chris is several years younger than the rest of the team – and they aren't all as sure of his skill in goal as his older brother is. . .

A fast-moving and realistic footballing story for young readers.

SBN 0 552 524514

THE BIG RACE

BY ROB CHILDS
ILLUSTRATED BY TIM MARWOOD

In one easy bound Andrew cleared the stream that trickled across the course. 'Great stuff!' shouted Chris. 'You're murdering them!' Andrew flashed him a grin. 'That's right. I'm going to win, like I said!'

But the race isn't going to be the piece of cake Andrew thinks. Unknown to the boys, the race meeting has attracted the attention of some very ruthless people and events are about to take a dramatic turn. . .

A fast-moving and realistic story for young readers from teacher Rob Childs, author of THE BIG MATCH and master of the sporting tale.

SBN 0 552 524611

STONE AGE MAGIC

BY BRIAN BALL
ILLUSTRATED BY MAUREEN BRADLEY

Class 3 are off to the Museum to see how Prehistoric Man once lived. When they find a magic machine there, they push the knobs and pull the levers – and bring two Stone Age children, Kinto and Canda, forward in time.

The Museum Director is delighted. His machine works! Now he wants to lock away the two Stone Age children so that he can study them properly. Billy, Ted and Sally know there is only thing they can do – run!

A hilarious new adventure for Class 3 – from the author of *Truant From Space*.

0 552 526037

If you would like to receive a Newsletter about our new Children's books, just fill in the coupon below with your name and address (or copy it onto a separate piece of paper if you don't want to spoil your book) and send it to:

The Children's Books Editor
Transworld Publishers Ltd.
61–63 Uxbridge Road,
Ealing
London W5 5SA

Please send me a Children's Newsletter:

Name . . . .

Address . . . .

. . . .

. . . .